Published by
Temperance Hall, Ltd.
Faubourg Marigny, New Orleans
1993

ISBN 0-9639525-0-1

Copyright Dalt Wonk 1993

Printed in the U.S.A.

on

acid free recycled paper

FOR
EUGENIE AND ERSY

She lived like a monarch in exile:
with nothing to claim, but her rank;
with nothing to prize, but her memories;
with nothing to give, but her thanks.
And somehow she always had flowers
(though people said she was in debt)
and her dresses were old, but exquisite
and her wings, you would never forget.
Sometimes he would watch her for hours
from the window of his restaurant.
When he waved, she'd pretend not to notice.
When he called, he would get no response.
But the sky was growing demented.
The wind was picking up speed.
The trees had begun to writhe and lament.
The clouds had begun to stampede.
So she entered and sat at a table.
He asked "Are you planning to dine?"
She said: "Just a pot of English tea
for the moment, if you don't mind."
And the rain clawed at the windows.
And the wind screamed in the trees.
"I can see that you are in trouble," he said,
giving her hand a squeeze.
"Why don't we make an arrangement,"
He winked a lascivious wink.
And flashing a thick wad of bills, he exclaimed:
"I'm not as bad as you think!"
And oh, his eyes were brutal!
And oh, his touch was warm!
She flew out the door in an instant
and vanished into the storm.
With nothing to gain, but her freedom.
With nothing to spend, but her force.
With nothing to save, but her honor.
With nothing to lose, but remorse.

MORAL:
Sometimes the greatest peril lies in safety.

# THE LIZARD AND THE FROG

On a steamy twilight in August,
Frog popped out of his pool.
He loved to take his evening stroll,
once it was dark and cool.
For all throughout the heat of the day,
he was forced to stay within,
or the air, that was hot as an oven,
would dry out his delicate skin.
He was taking some liquid refreshment
at a barroom in the vicinity,
when his eyes met the eyes of the lizard
like dark emerald pools of infinity.
"You'll take your ease at the water's edge.
I'll watch you from the pool.
And join you when the sun goes down,
and the air is moist and cool.
For though we love each other,
we can not live as one.
You'd perish in my liquid home
as I would in the sun."

The courtyard is fragrant with blossoms.
They walk down the aisle in a trance
through the flickering glow of the gas lights,
through the shadows that quiver and dance.

She wears a borrowed pearl necklace
and a veil that's blue for good luck
and a little woven coronet
of flowers— newly plucked.
But, silently, she slips away
at the height of the celebration,
while he is laughing with some friends
and accepting congratulations.
She hurries to the lily pond—
where the stars are all adrift:
to join him in his element
will be her wedding gift.

# MISS DACHSHUND WALKS HOME

The Opera Guild had been unspeakably boring,
so Miss Dachshund decided to walk and take some air —
shrugging off a chorus of dire warnings.
She, for one, refused to live in fear.
The streets were empty. The night was hot and damp,
with the strangled breath of some expended storm.
Buzzing insects swarmed around the lamps
that formed a line of beacons to guide her home,
but oh the long dark shadows in between,
each like a dangerous passage she must risk,
where who knows what malefactor lurked unseen.
Involuntarily, her pace grew brisk.
And then, as though her fears had taken shape,
she thought she detected — though she had to squint —
a scruffy mongrel lounging on a stoop,
who eyed her with a predatory glint.
She had barely time enough to repent her folly,
when he loomed before her and her way was barred.
Then, in a speech that was commendably terse,
he gave her to understand he'd like her purse.
"But _that_ was the gift of an admiring collie
I used to stroll with on the boulevard,"
she whimpered, whisking the token from his grasp,
as though his very touch would leave it fouled.
He signalled his impatience with a growl
and started pawing at her diamond clasp.
"Not that!" she sobbed "It was my mother's mother's."
Nothing was left to steal, but her string of pearls!
"These once belonged," she started to explain . . .
(his eyes turned slits, his lips grew flecked with slaver)
. . . to someone dear to me, but now they're yours."
And surrendering, with a submissive smile,
the necklace to it's crude inheritor,
she hurried on her homeward way again.

MORAL:
Much trouble can be averted
by knowing when to stop.

# THE MOCKINGBIRD AND THE PIGEON

From dawn to dusk, the Pigeon would go begging,
trying to win his crust of daily bread
and he made his pitch by endlessly repeating
the only tune he carried in his head.

But though he lacked extraordinary talents,
one important lesson he had learned
on the city streets, which were his Alma Mater:
"Thou shalt not fear to take what others earn."

And any time there was a prize disputed,
to the center of the melee, he would charge;
for he was blessed with an imposing stature,
and the small must always flee before the large.

One afternoon, when he was out inspecting
a sector of the pavement he controlled,
above the noisy humdrum of the traffic,
he heard a voice that beckoned and consoled.

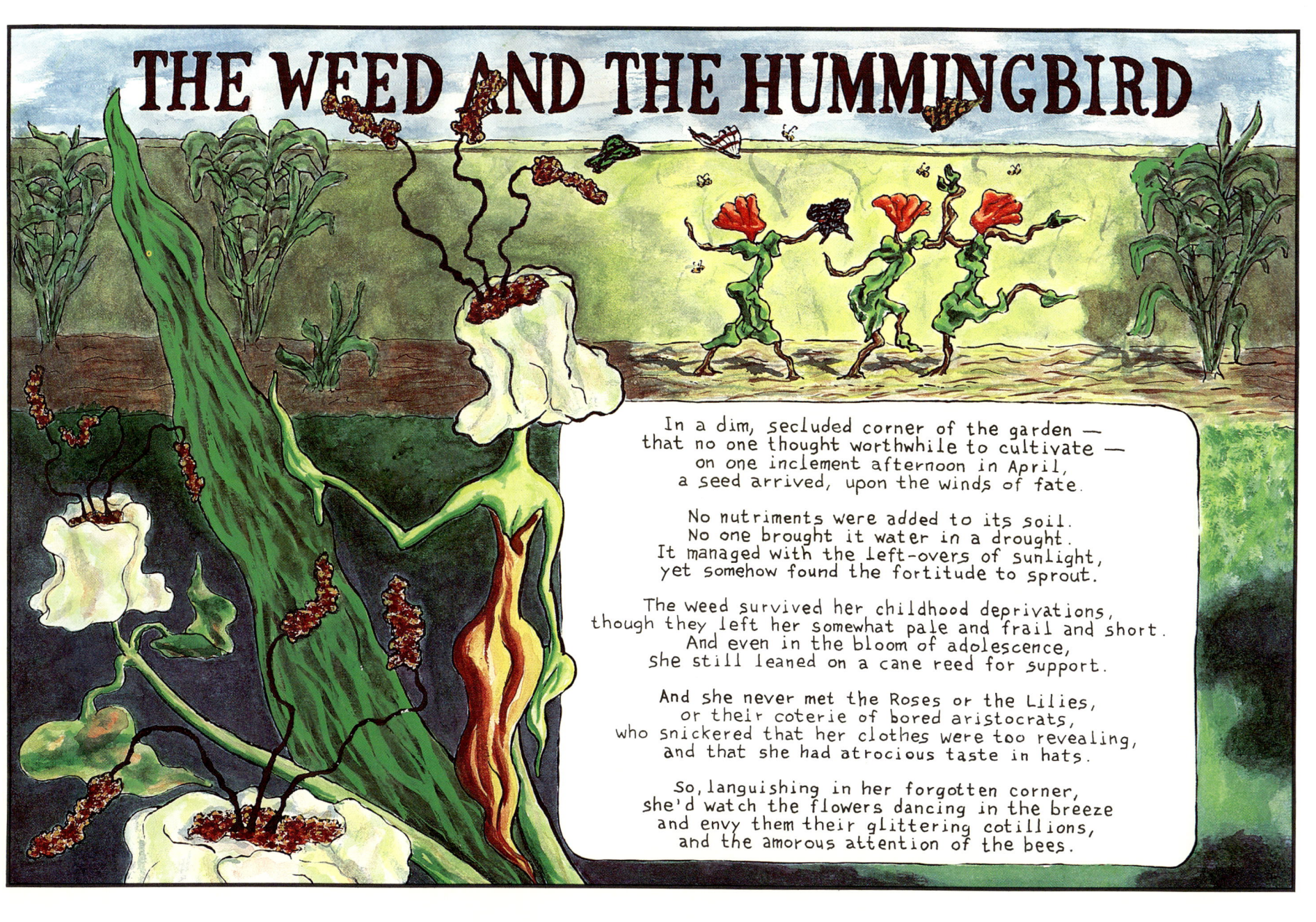

"Since I am small, I never will be noticed.
Since I am weak, I don't deserve respect.
I get no help, because I am not worthy.
I am alone, because I can't connect."

One day, while thus lamenting her exclusion,
she heard a soft, perplexing sort of hum,
then glimpsed the most extraordinary creature,
floating over the chrysanthemums —

floating, with his air of connoisseurship
and his minute sartorial perfection,
floating with the fragilest of movements,
miraculous to say, in her direction.

She offered up her fragrance to refresh him.
She yielded him her nectar and he sipped.
With the smoothness of her petals, she caressed him—
thankful for his brief companionship.

In the morning, when she woke, he was beside her.
From day to day, his departure was delayed.
And she, who was so conscious of her failings,
could not refrain from asking why he stayed.

"Since you are small, you've learned how to be pliant
Since you are weak, you've learned to comprehend.
You get no help, so you've grown self-reliant.
Since you're alone, you've learned to be a friend."

MORAL:
See yourself the way your friends see you.

Special thanks to:

my mother, Ruth Cohen
my cousin, Bob Preiskel
Steven Bingler
Linda Usdin
Tina Freeman
Nancy Moss
Julian Mutter
Tom Varisco
Charles Nelson
Carol Flake
Peregrine Whittlesey
Roland Chiara
Mr. and Mrs J. C. Martin, Jr.
Rebecca Avery


and also:
Vittorio
Cinzia
Blair
Jon
Henri
The Society of Saint Anne


But, above all,
to my exacting muses,
Iris and Josephine.